The Riddle of the
OOGLIE BOOGLIE

by Carole Marsh

About the Three Amigos

Weng-Ho, Grant, and Seve are best friends. Weng-Ho is 7. Grant is 8. Seve is 9.

They live on the same street. Weng-Ho lives next door to Grant. Grant lives next door to Seve.

They go to the same school. Weng-Ho's classroom is next to Grant's. Grant's classroom is next to Seve's.

They each have a younger or older sister. Weng-Ho has a baby sister. Grant has an older sister. Seve has an even older sister.

They ride the school bus together. They eat lunch together. They go to recess together. Sometimes they get in trouble together. They like to solve riddles, mysteries, and puzzles together.

Or, at least they like to try!

BOOKS IN THIS SERIES

TABLE OF CONTENTS

The Riddle of the

OOGLIE
BOOGLIE

by Carole Marsh

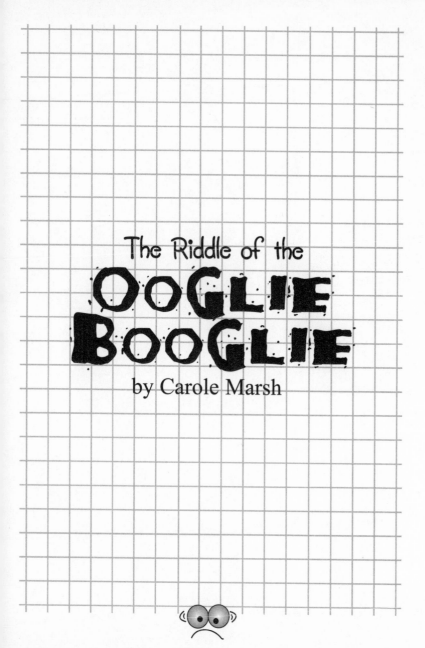

A STRANGE NEW FRIEND

Grant, Weng-Ho, and Seve liked to meet new friends. However, they were a little surprised when Grant's Mom took them to spend the afternoon with Professor O. B. Peterson.

For one thing, Professor Peterson was old. If the boys had to have a "babysitter" (a term they did not like), then they preferred that it be someone

young and fun. You know, like Uncle
Michael, who had lots of technology around
his house…like games to play.

But Professor Peterson did not have a fun
house. He had a strange, boring apartment.
For one thing, all the walls were brown.
For another, all the furniture was old and
uncomfortable. Uncle Michael had comfy
beanbag chairs to sit in.

Uncle Michael's house was also noisy.
He played cool music and had an electronic
guitar. Professor Peterson's house was way
too quiet.

"It sounds like dead people live here,"
Grant noted as he sat on a lumpy
brown sofa.

"I don't hear any dead people," Weng-Ho
said. He darted his eyes left and right. He

did not want to see any dead people
for sure!

"Grant means that it's as quiet as a
tomb," Seve explained. "Like the Day of
the Dead."

Grant squirmed on the lumpy brown
sofa. "What's the Day of the Dead?"
he asked.

Seve squirmed too. He sat on a bumpy
footstool Professor Peterson called an
ottoman. "It's a Hispanic holiday."

"You celebrate dead people?" Weng-Ho
asked. He
looked very
surprised and
confused.

"No," said
Seve. "We

celebrate that they lived. There are cool costumes and special bread to eat. I guess you'd just have to be there to understand."

Weng-Ho sighed and squirmed. He sat on the hard brown floor. "I guess I'd rather be at the Day of the Dead than here this afternoon," he said sadly.

"Me, too," said Grant.

"Me, too," said Seve.

Soon, Professor Peterson came into the room. He entered the room from a strange metal door. It looked like it could be the door to Frankenstein's house. It was made of heavy gray metal with rivets in it. The door had a small round porthole window at the very top with thick glass with a wire grid inside. In fact, the thick glass looked

5

like the glass in Professor Peterson's eyeglasses.

"Hello, boys," the professor said. "I'm so glad you came to stay with me this afternoon."

Grant thought that the professor did not sound glad at all. He knew that the professor was his Mom's friend. His Mom had to go to work on urgent business, she said… "At the last minute."

"Can't you take us with you?" Grant had asked.

"No," his Mom had said. "I can't take you where I'm going. But I have arranged for you to stay with Professor Peterson. I promise I will be back soon."

Seve and Weng-Ho had to come along too because their Moms were at work.

Grant was glad he was not here in the brown lumpy house with the big metal door with the thick glass all alone. He was sort of afraid of Professor Peterson.

"You can sit here if you like," said the professor. "I have things to read over there." He motioned to a shabby bookcase with lots of tattered old magazines on it.

"Or, you can go in my kitchen and have some water to drink if you like." Then the professor turned on his heels and went through the metal door, which closed behind him with a chilly

WHOOSH.

"Oh, great!" said Grant after the professor disappeared. "We get to look at boring old magazines and drink water."

"This is sort of like jail," said Seve.

"It's worse than prison," said Weng-Ho. "Prison has television."

The other two boys looked all around.

No Television!

Grant got up and walked over and looked at one of the magazines. "These are medical journals," he said. "I guess Professor Peterson is a doctor."

"I wonder what kind of doctor he is," said Seve.

Weng-Ho looked at one of the journal covers. It had a skeleton on it. "I think he is a Day of the Dead doctor!"

The boys quietly went and sat back down on the lumpy furniture and hard floor. Soon they got thirsty.

"I just have to have a drink of water," said Grant.

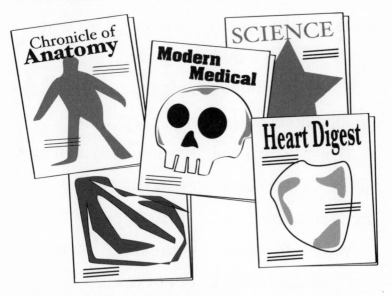

"Me, too," said Weng-Ho.

"Me, too," said Seve.

The three boys got up and tiptoed into

the tiny kitchen. There was a little sink and a little refrigerator and a little stove. Three glasses sat on the counter; they were dusty.

"I don't think Professor Peterson drinks much water," Grant noted.

"I wonder what he does drink?" Seve asked.

"Bug juice," said Weng-Ho.

That made the boys giggle. At first they giggled quietly, then they giggled louder.

"Hush!" Seve finally said. "I would rather the professor stay in that room with the metal door. Let's drink some water."

Weng-Ho looked all around. "Do we get it out of the faucet or out of the refrigerator?"

The boys looked at the sink. Then they looked at the refrigerator.

"I think we should go for cool water from the refrigerator," suggested Grant.

"Do you think it's ok to open the professor's refrigerator?" Weng-Ho asked hesitantly.

"He didn't say we couldn't," said Seve. He reached up and opened the door.

The three boys looked inside. At the same time, they all said,

"UGGGGGGG!"

"YUUUUUUUCK!"

the boys cried.

"What is that gross stuff?" asked Seve.

"It looks like Mom's leftovers,"
said Grant.

"Then I would not eat at your house!"
said Weng-Ho.

"You eat at my house all the time," Grant
reminded his friend.

Inside the refrigerator sat a variety of jars
and other containers.

One large jar was filled with creepy-crawly little white bugs. The label on the jar said **MAGGOTS.**

Another jar was stuffed with some slick, black slug-looking things. The label read **LEECHES.**

A container on the lower shelf looked like it was full of fishing worms. A label on that container said **WHIPWORMS.**

A fourth container held a vile-looking liquid called **VENOM.**

"Isn't venom that stuff poisonous snakes spit out?" Weng-Ho asked.

"I think so," said Seve.

"Look at that jar on the bottom shelf," said Grant. He pointed his trembling finger at a small jar labeled **BAT SALIVA.**

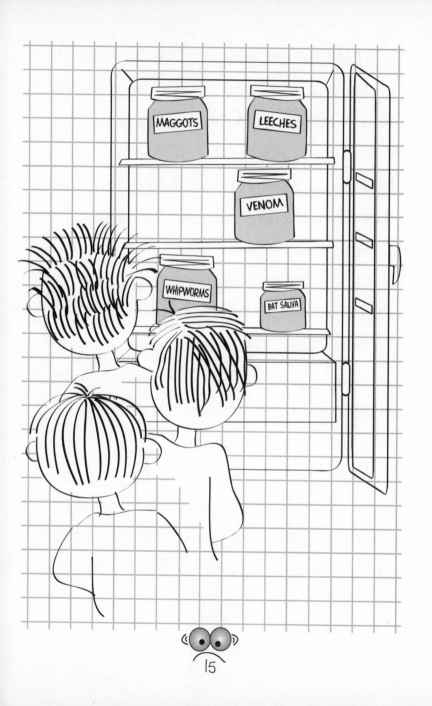

"Isn't saliva like spit?" asked Weng-Ho.

"I think it is," said Seve, swallowing hard.

The boys stood quietly for a moment. Cool air from the inside of the refrigerator blew out on them and made the tiny, little hairs on their forearms stand up like frozen grass.

"I don't think I'm thirsty anymore," said Grant.

"Me either," Weng-Ho agreed.

"And I know I do NOT want to eat lunch here!" said Seve, holding his stomach. His face looked a little green.

Suddenly they heard a shuffling behind them and the boys jumped. Before they could slam the refrigerator door and spin around, a voice behind them said, "Would you like a snack, boys?"

"No thank you!" the three amigos cried together.

They turned around to see Professor Peterson standing there in his white lab coat. He reached his wrinkled hand in his pocket and pulled out…three packs of peanut butter crackers, which he handed to the boys.

"There are some sodas in the cooler over there," the professor said. He pointed to a foam cooler under the sink.

The boys took the crackers and moved into a huddle by the sink. As they cowered there, the professor opened the refrigerator door. He looked at the jars and smiled. Then he looked at the boys and smiled.

18

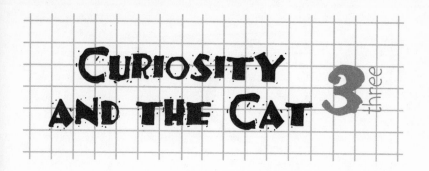

CURIOSITY AND THE CAT 3 three

Fearfully, the boys opened the cooler. Sure enough there were cans of soda nestled in ice in the cooler. They each grabbed a drink and headed for the living room. They sat together on the brown, lumpy sofa and opened their crackers. As they ate and drank they stared at the big metal door.

"I wonder what he is doing in there?" Grant said.

"Me, too," said Seve.

"Maybe we don't want to know," said Weng-Ho. "Maybe this is a riddle that we don't really want to solve?"

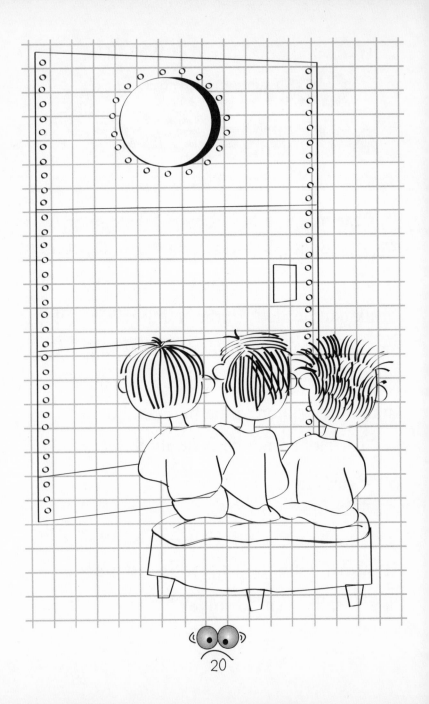

20

Grant and Seve stared at Weng-Ho.

"We always want to solve a riddle, puzzle, or mystery—don't we?" said Grant.

Weng-Ho shrugged. "Sure," he said. "Always."

Suddenly, the metal door swung open and Professor Peterson bolted into the living room. "I have to run out for a moment," he said. His voice sounded very urgent. "You ooglie booglie boys stay right here until I get back!" Then the professor ran out the door, his lab coat flying.

"What did he call us?" said Seve.

Grant giggled. "I think he called us ooglie booglie?"

"What's an ooglie booglie?" asked Weng-Ho. "I do not think I am an ooglie booglie."

"How do you know if you don't know

21

what an ooglie booglie is?" Seve asked.

"I don't know," said Weng-Ho."

"Well, I know that he should have not left us here by ourselves. Mom will not like that."

For a moment the three amigos were very quiet.

Finally Weng-Ho said, "We're all alone."

"Yeah," said Seve, "all alone."

There was more silence, then Grant said, "Well, what are we waiting for?!"

The boys jumped up and headed for the big metal door!

After they dashed through the door, they froze in place. The room was a real laboratory. It looked more like a research lab than a medical lab where you might treat patients. However, what it REALLY looked like was a madman's laboratory—at least to the three amigos.

"What is all this stuff?" Weng-Ho said.

"I don't know," said Grant, "but at least there aren't any bodies in here…or none that I can see. And I don't plan to go any further."

Seve looked like he might throw up. "I think we should go back into the living room, sit on the brown, lumpy sofa, finish our snack, and hope your Mom comes to pick us up REAL SOON."

The boys turned to do just that, but before they could even spin around, they heard the big, metal door creak behind them! *CREEEEEEK*

CREEPY-CRAWLY MEDICINE 4 four

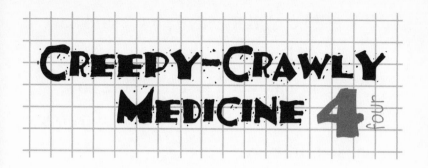

"Aha!" said Professor O. B. Peterson as he entered the laboratory. "I had a feeling that you three boys could not resist taking a peek at my work area."

Grant, Weng-Ho, and Seve froze in place. Their skin was pale but their cheeks were red.

"We hope you're not angry," said Grant. "We just got curious. We didn't touch anything."

25

"We'll be glad to leave now," said Seve with great sincerity.

"Yes, I think we'll just be going now," Weng-Ho agreed. The three boys took one giant step forward.

"Oh, no!" said the professor with a roar of a laugh.

HA! HA! HA! HA! HA! HA! HA!

"I love ooglie booglie little boys. I eat them for lunch!"

The frightened boys shook in their sneakers. They did not know what being an ooglie booglie was, but they knew that they did not want to be the professor's lunch!

26

"Isn't there anything we can do…to get out of here?" Grant begged. "It's very interesting, but I think we'd better…"

Before Grant could finish his sentence, the professor interrupted him. "Oh, no," the professor said. "Now we are going to have some fun."

Grant, Weng-Ho, and Seve looked at one another nervously. They were pretty sure that they did not want to have fun in this chilly, creepy laboratory with a professor who called them ooglie booglie and wanted to eat them for lunch.

The professor shoved the boys toward a metal table. "This is a test," the professor said. "If you can figure out the answers, I will let you go."

"We aren't very good at tests," Seve

admitted. "Plus, we haven't had a chance to study, you know…sir."

The professor ignored him.

"LOOK!" the professor said. "What do you see?"

Grant looked down at a metal tray the professor had put on the metal table. "It looks like a dead squirrel."

"It sure smells like a dead squirrel," Seve agreed, wrinkling his nose.

"It's a rotten dead squirrel," Weng-Ho said.

"EXACTLY!" shouted the professor. "Stay right here!"

The professor left the room. The boys were too afraid to move. Their knees quivered like Jell-O® Jigglers.® Suddenly, the professor returned with one of the jars from the refrigerator. It held the little squirmy things.

"Do you know what these are?" the professor asked. He held the jar close to their faces for the boys to inspect.

"Maggots?" guessed Grant since the label said **MAGGOTS.**

"RIGHT!" said the professor. And without further ado, he dumped the jar of maggots onto the rotting squirrel flesh.

The boys were astounded to see the maggots gobbling up the dead flesh until the squirrel looked like new. Well, almost like new.

"I think I might throw up," warned Seve.

"NONSENSE!" cried the professor. "Please do not regurgitate in my lab. Instead, tell me what just happened."

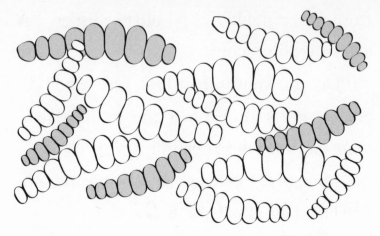

"Well, you grossed us out," said Grant.

"Oh, besides that," the professor said merrily as if he were having lots of fun.

Grant was afraid not to answer. "Well, the maggots ate the dead flesh."

"YES!" said the professor. "And how do you think this could help a human being."

"I have a guess," said Seve. "If the maggots eat the dead flesh, it might help the person not get an infection or something bad like that."

"VERY GOOD!" said the professor. "A nasty infection could cause someone to lose a finger, or an arm, or a foot, or a leg, you know."

"Now, I think I'm gonna…" Weng-Ho began, then stopped. "You know," he said. "That's pretty interesting."

"So these are good maggots?" Grant asked.

"Medical maggots," said the professor. Then he ran out of the room toward the refrigerator.

"Uh, oh," said Weng-Ho.

In a few minutes the professor returned. "Come on over to this table," he order the boys. "Take a look!"

The boys obeyed.

The professor dumped the jar of
LEECHES onto a tray. "Now what
do you think these are for?" he asked.

"To be gross?" said Seve.

"To be ugly?" said Weng-Ho.

Grant looked thoughtful. "I think they
might could be used in medicine, too, but I
don't know how. I know leeches can grab
hold of your leg if you are in water, like in
a jungle or something. They suck
your blood."

"I think…" started Weng-Ho. He looked
a little green.

The professor interrupted. "I think you
are very smart!" he said to Grant. "Today,
we use medical leeches to drain the blood
from some types of wounds. The leeches
drain excess fluid. Their saliva stops blood

clotting and helps circulation."

"So leeches are cool?" Seve asked.

"Leeches are very COOL!" said the
professor. And then he ran right back out of
the room.

"Oh, no," said Weng-Ho.

In a moment, the professor returned. The
boys were not surprised to see the third
container from the refrigerator. The
professor led the boys to a third table. He

poured the contents of the third jar onto a metal tray. **"PIG WHIPWORMS!"** he said proudly.

"Yep," said Grant. "They're worms, all right." The little, squiggly worms squirmed around.

"How do you treat sick people with these?" Seve bravely asked.

"Well, first they have to swallow them!" said the professor.

Weng-Ho looked a lot green, but he

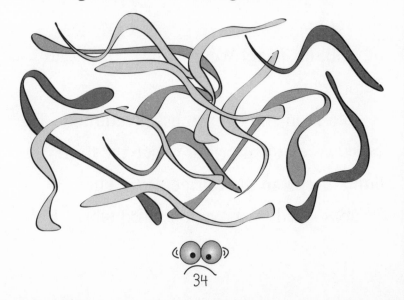

surprised his friends by saying, "I think…I think…I think I know why. Can they help people with sick guts?"

"WONDERFUL!" said the professor. "They can indeed. "They are used to treat people who have problems with their intestines."

The three amigos just stared at the professor. They waited for the professor to go and get the other jars they had seen from the refrigerator.

When he did not, Grant hinted, "What other kinds of weird things do you use to help people?"

The professor looked delighted to be asked. "Snake venom can help people who have had strokes. And bat spit, too."

"Bat spit?" said Seve.

"Poisonous snakes?" said Weng-Ho.

"Is all this old-fashioned medicine like people use to use a long time ago?" Grant guessed.

Professor O. B. Peterson laughed. "You kids are pretty smart. Some of this is old-fashioned. But doctors are finding that what is old is new again—and we can make it work better than ever."

"I always thought medicine was boring," said Seve.

"I thought going to the doctor was the worst thing in the world," Weng-Ho agreed.

"I thought treating people just meant pills and shots, not cool, yucky stuff like bat spit and leeches and maggots and worms," said Grant. "I like gross stuff. Maybe I will grow up and become a doctor one day.

Mom would like that."

"I thought you wanted to be a detective," said Seve.

Grant thought about that. "I do. But this is sort of like being a doctor detective. That would be a cool job."

"I THINK SO!" said the professor. He laughed very loudly.

The boys looked at him. Either he was very smart, they thought. Or, maybe he was some kind of mad scientist. He was just a riddle that they could not solve.

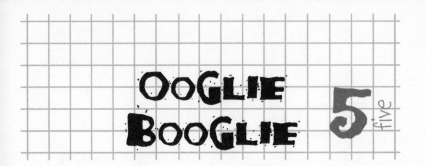

OOGLIE BOOGLIE 5

Grant began to inch his way toward the metal door. The other boys followed. The professor looked disappointed. He followed the boys. They did not know if he was going to open the door for them...or maybe make them stay inside. Maybe he wanted to try out some of his medicine on them.

There was another riddle Grant just couldn't figure out. "Why did you call us ooglie booglies?" he asked the professor.

This time the professor did not laugh. "When I was a boy your age," he said, "kids made fun of me because I was

interested in weird things like maggots and leeches. It hurt my feelings. They called me an ugly boy. The more they said it, it came out like ooglie booglie."

The boys looked puzzled. They felt a little sorry for the lonesome professor.

"After I grew up and became a doctor, I was proud of what I had learned. But because some people are very squeamish about such things, I called my little maggot and leech and worm friends ooglie booglies."

"Soooo, you are calling us maggots?" Grant asked. His feelings were hurt.

"Or leeches?" said Seve. His feelings were hurt.

"Or pig worms?" asked Weng-Ho. His feelings were hurt.

"NO!" said the professor, startling the boys. "I call my friends ooglie booglies, whether that's bats and snakes…or boys."

"OHHHH!" said the boys together. They were very relieved.

Suddenly they all jumped when there was a

RAP·RAP·RAP

on the door. The door screeched open and

there stood Grant's Mom.

"Have my little ooglie booglie boys behaved?" she asked the professor.

The professor laughed. "These three amigos have been very good. Not one worm or maggot or leech is missing."

"You know about ooglie booglie?!" Grant asked his Mom. He was so surprised.

"Sure," she said. "When I was in the professor's class, it was an honor to be called an ooglie booglie."

The three amigos laughed. They had made a surprising new friend, lots of surprising new friends.

"Oh, by the way," said Grant, as they started to leave. "I noticed that your initials are O. B. Does that stand for ooglie booglie?"

The professor shook his head sadly. "I WISH!" he said. "Unfortunately, my mother named me Obidiah Baltimore."

"Oh, brother," said Weng-Ho. "Oogli Boogli is a lot better than that."

The boys laughed. So did Mom. And so did the professor, who did not look so lonesome now that he had three new amigo friends.

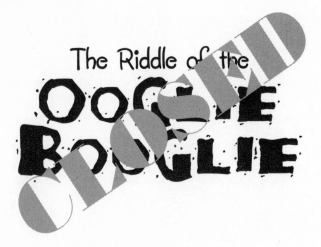

ABOUT THE SERIES CREATOR

Carole Marsh writes lots of books for kids. She started writing when she was just a kid. She is married to a cowboy named Bob. She likes to read books about science and medicine. She likes to figure out riddles, puzzles, and mysteries. Grant is her real-life grandson. Weng-Ho and Seve are his real-life amigos!

TALK ABOUT IT!

1. Who are the main characters in this story? Who is your favorite character? Why?

2. Why do you think Mom let Professor O.B. Peterson babysit the three amigos?

3. When you first met the professor in the story, how did you feel about him? By the end of the story, how did you feel about the professor?

4. What did you think was in the refrigerator? What did you think was behind the big, metal Frankenstein-like door?

TALK ABOUT IT!

5. Which parts of the story do you think the author made up? Which parts do you believe are actual facts, if any?

6. Which character was the bravest? Smartest? Funniest? Scaredist?

7. If you could be helped by maggots, leeches, worms, bats, or snakes, would you be willing to undertake such a treatment? Why or why not?

8. What do you think the three amigos learned during their unusual afternoon in the laboratory?

BRING IT TO LIFE!

1. Create a "play" from this story. Select students to be characters. Set the "stage" with three areas for the living room, kitchen, and laboratory. Find props. (You can use rice for maggots, black balloons for leeches, and gummi worms for the worms.) Rehearse your parts. Perform the play for fellow students, the school, or at home for your family!

2. Scavenger Hunt!: Find a picture and some information of a maggot, leech, pig worm (or other type of worm), bat, and venomous snake.

BRING IT TO LIFE!

3. Bring in a guest speaker! Have a local doctor come in and talk about how some medical methods used in the story once were "old -fashioned," went out of fashion, and now are in use again.

4. Take a field trip!: Find a lab you can visit where you can see medical maggots, leeches, and worms. (Your teacher will love it!)

5. See if you can research and find out what other unusual medical "miracles" are happening right now. [Hint: finger or limb reattachment; bionic body parts; laser operations.]

GLOSSARY

amigo: Spanish word for friend

laboratory: place where a scientist works

larvae: one stage in the development of an insect

leech: bloodsucking worm

maggot: fly larvae

regurgitate: to vomit or "throw up"

rivets: metal bolts

venom: poisonous fluid from a snake or other creature

TECH CONNECTS

Hey, Kids! Visit
www.carolemarshmysteries.com to:

JOIN THE CAROLE MARSH
MYSTERIES FAN CLUB!

LEARN MORE ABOUT
CREEPY-CRAWLY MEDICINE

GET AN OOGLI BOOGLI
WORD SEARCH